CAMILA

THE RECORD-BREAKER

written by ALICIA SALAZAR

illustrated by THAIS DAMIÃO

PICTURE WINDOW BOOKS

a capstone imprint

Camila the Star is published by Picture Window Books,
an imprint of Capstone.
1710 Roe Crest Drive
North Mankato, Minnesota 56003
www.capstonepub.com

Library of Congress Cataloging-in-Publication Data
Names: Salazar, Alicia, 1973– author. | Damiao, Thais, illustrator.
Title: Camila the record-breaking star / by Alicia Salazar; illustrated byThais Damiao.
Description: North Mankato, Minnesota : Picture Window Books, a Capstone imprint,
[2021] | Series: Camila the star | Audience: Ages 5–7. | Audience: Grades K–1. |
Summary: Camila dreams of being a star and, after learning about children who break
world records, decides she will do the same--but how? Includes glossary, glossary of
Spanish words, activities, and discussion questions.
Identifiers: LCCN 2020025175 (print) | LCCN 2020025176 (ebook) |
ISBN 9781515882121 (library binding) | ISBN 9781515883210 (paperback) |
ISBN 9781515891826 (pdf)
Subjects: CYAC: World records—Fiction. | Ability—Fiction. | Family life—Fiction. |
Hispanic Americans—Fiction.
Classification: LCC PZ7.1.S2483 Cam 2021 (print) | LCC PZ7.1.S2483 (ebook) | DDC
[E]—dc23
LC record available at https://lccn.loc.gov/2020025175
LC ebook record available at https://lccn.loc.gov/2020025176

Designer: Kay Fraser

TABLE OF CONTENTS

Meet Camila and Her Family

Papá

Mamá

Ana, age 14

Andres, age 10

Camila, age 7

Spanish Glossary

canción (kahn-SYOHN)—song

extraordinario (ehks-trah-or-dee-NAH-ryoh)—extraordinary

Mamá (mah-MAH)—Mom

mercado (mehr-KAH-doh)—market

panaderia (pah-nah-deh-REE-ah)—bakery

Papá (pah-PAH)—Dad

que chido (KEH CHEE-doh)—how awesome

una estrella (OO-nah es-TREH-yah)—a star

Chapter 1

THE MAGAZINE COVER

For as long as she could remember, Camila wanted to be famous. She wanted to be **una estrella**. She just didn't know how she would do it yet.

"Class, I would like you to read the cover story of *Star Student* magazine," said her teacher, Mrs. Jolly.

Camila jumped out of her seat when she read it!

The kid on the cover broke a world record. He built the tallest block tower ever!

When she got home, Camila skipped into the family room.

"I am going to break a world record! I'll be a star on the cover of magazines!" she said.

"¡Que chido!" said Mamá.

"Which world record are you going to break?" asked Papá.

"Something extraordinario," Camila said with a twirl.

Chapter 2

BREAKING A RECORD

Camila and her brother,
Andres, looked up other young
world-record holders. They
found some clever entries.

"All I have to do is break one
of their records," said Camila.
"Then I'll be a star!"

She tried drawing as many

cats as she could for one minute.

But it took her one whole

minute just to draw the face.

"I'll still be a star!" she said.

She tried balancing the
most bottles on one finger.
But the bottles kept falling.

"I'll still be a star!" she said.

She tried catching the most
lemons blindfolded.

But she kept dropping the
lemons.

"I'll never be a star," she
said with a sigh.

Camila sat down with her
head in her hands. Then her
brain lit up. She sat up straight.

"I don't want to break
someone else's record," said
Camila. "I want to set my own
record!"

Camila thought about the things she was really good at doing. She was good at singing. And she was good at writing songs.

Camila decided she would write her own song.

"I will be the youngest person to get 1,000 plays on SongCloud," she said.

Camila and Mamá made sure no kid had done it before. Then they signed Camila up on the World Record website.

Chapter 3

A SPECIAL SONG

"It has to be a special **canción**," said Camila as she prepared to write.

"What things are special to you?" asked Papá.

Camila made a list of everything that was special to her.

Family.

Being a star.

Her cat, Angel.

When she thought of Angel, she heard a tune in her head. She wrote and sang and sang and wrote.

The first song was too fast.
The second one had no rhythm.
Camila tried again and again
until . . .

"Myyyy caaaat is all thaaat!"
she sang.

Andres helped her record her song on the computer. They uploaded it to SongCloud.

Camila crossed her fingers for good luck.

One week went by, and she had only five plays. Another week passed, and she had just twenty plays.

"Maybe I'm not star material," said Camila as she sank into a chair.

Finally, on the third week, she signed onto SongCloud and saw:
"MY CAT IS ALL THAT" – 1,200 PLAYS

"You are a star now!" cheered her family.

"Not yet!" said Camila. "I have to be on a magazine cover!"

Ana, Camila's older sister, surprised her the next day. She made a magazine cover with Camila's picture. Ana and Andres taped up copies at the **panaderia** and the **mercado**.

"I'm officially a star now!" said Camila with a smile as bright as the sun. "Maybe next my song will go number one!"

Who Will Hold the Record?

Do you dream of setting a world record like Camila? Why not start practicing in a friendly competition with your friends? Who will hold the records in these two penny games?

SUPPLIES
30 pennies per person

ACTIVITY 1
STACK THE PENNIES

1. Place each person's pennies in front of them at a table or counter.

2. Set a timer for 15 seconds.

3. Using just one hand, see how many pennies you can stack in 15 seconds. To make it extra challenging, use your less dominant hand. (That's the one you *don't* use to write!)

4. Whoever stacks the most pennies holds the record!

ACTIVITY 2
SPIN THE PENNIES

1. Take a minute or two to practice spinning a penny on its side.

2. When everyone feels ready, each person should take a turn spinning pennies. The goal is to see how many pennies you can spin at once.

3. Whoever spins the most pennies at once holds the record!

Glossary

blindfolded (BLIND-fohld-ed)—having the eyes covered

clever (KLEV-er)—showing a lot of imagination

famous (FAY-mus)—very well-known

rhythm (RITH-uhm)—a pattern of beats

star material (STAHR muh-TEER-ee-uhl)—having traits and skills that make a person a good performer

uploaded (UHP-lohd-ed)—to transfer information from one computer to another

Think About the Story

1. Camila tried to break a few different records. Which record do you think was the most challenging? Explain your answer.

2. Imagine you were on the cover of *Star Student* magazine. What would be your claim to fame? Draw your own cover and write what would make you famous.

3. Camila listed things that were special to her. Write a list of five things that are special to you. Then choose one thing and write a sentence about what makes it special.

About the Author

Alicia Salazar is a Mexican American children's book author who has written for blogs, magazines, and educational publishers. She was also once an elementary school teacher and a marine biologist. She currently lives in the suburbs of Houston, Texas, but is a city girl at heart. When Alicia is not dreaming up new adventures to experience, she is turning her adventures into stories for kids.

About the Illustrator

Thais Damião is a Brazilian illustrator and graphic designer. Born and raised in a small city in Rio de Janeiro, Brazil, she spent her childhood playing with her brother and cousins and drawing all the time. Her illustrations are dedicated to children and inspired by nature and friendship. Thais currently lives in California.